IN THE SHADOW
OF AN EAGLE

IN THE SHADOW OF AN EAGLE

AND OTHER ADVENTURE STORIES
Compiled by the Editors
of
Highlights for Children

BOYDS MILLS PRESS

Compilation copyright © 1992 by Boyds Mills Press, Inc.
Contents copyright by Highlights for Children, Inc.
All rights reserved
Published by Boyds Mills Press, Inc.
A Highlights Company
815 Church Street
Honesdale, Pennsylvania 18431
Printed in the United States of America

Publisher Cataloging-in-Publication Data
Main entry under title :
    In the shadow of an eagle : and other adventure stories / compiled by
the Editors of Highlights for Children.
[96] p. : ill. ; cm.
Stories originally published in *Highlights for Children*.
Summary: A collection of adventure stories for young people.
ISBN 1-56397-078-3
[1. Adventure stories.] I. Highlights for Children. II. Title.
        [F]   1992
Library of Congress Catalog Card Number 91-77001

Drawings by Judith Hunt

        13 14 15 16 17 18 19 20

Highlights is a registered trademark of Highlights for Children, Inc.

CONTENTS

In the Shadow of an Eagle

By Sally Gwin

Winter was over, the rivers ran free, and Anna's traps had yielded several squirrels. Proudly she reached up to her neck to touch the sun-warmed pelts that hung from a leather thong on her backpack.

Anna had been leading a reindeer sled since she was seven. She had been sewing skin boots and mittens since she was ten. She had been herding reindeer for as long as she could remember, but only now that she was twelve had she been allowed to set her own traps.

Anna's parents had come to Alaska from Lapland before Anna was born. They had come to teach the Eskimos how to herd reindeer. In turn, Anna's family had learned many skills from the Eskimos.

New green tundra grasses shone in the sun, and the world felt good. At first Anna was hardly aware of the whir and flap above her head. But when a darkness blocked the sun, she looked up to see an enormous eagle hovering above her. His wings, nearly six feet wide, threw a shadow over her. His black eyes seemed to glint like river pebbles as he stared down at Anna. Suddenly he swooped; his knife-sharp talons, curled in menace, missed her head by inches. Anna threw up her arms, warding off the attack. She had heard Eskimo legends of eagles carrying children off to their nests, but she had never heard of it actually happening.

As quickly as he had come, the menacing bird was gone. And just as quickly the eagle reappeared, as if by magic, out of the cloudless sky, swooping, gliding, sliding straight for Anna, and then up and away.

"It must be my squirrels he's after," Anna

murmured. She stopped to stuff the animal pelts into her backpack. "I guess it wasn't me he wanted for his lunch after all." Anna laughed nervously. The sound of her laugh was loud in the vast, quiet tundra, where the only other sound was the lapping of the water in a lake nearby.

As Anna searched the sky and the horizon for her attacker, she saw a dark spot over by the lake. "Now what is that?"

The eagle reappeared, sliding down the sky toward the dark spot. At first Anna was relieved that he seemed to have found a new interest. Then she grew curious.

The ground around the lake was swampy as the tundra thawed in the spring sun. Anna's deerhide boots stuffed with river grasses kept her feet warm and dry, but she stepped carefully anyway. Sometimes you could sink deep in the wet muskeg.

As Anna got closer to the dark spot, she saw that it was some kind of animal. Anna couldn't understand why it didn't get up and run away. It was too large to be easy prey for the eagle. As she came near it, she understood. There, curled in a soft, quivering ball, was a reindeer calf, probably no more than a week old.

As she approached, the eagle dived again. His talons outstretched, he grabbed at the calf. Anna shrieked and ran straight toward the flapping wings. "Let go!" she screamed.

Surprised by the rush of his human attacker, the bird let go. He soared upward. "And don't come back," Anna yelled, shaking an angry fist.

"You poor orphan. He was trying to scare me off so he could have you. He *will* have you, too, if I leave you here." The eagle had made two tiny puncture wounds in the calf's soft back. Anna gently stroked his ears. "What are we going to do?"

The calf looked at her with big black eyes. As she stroked him, he stopped quivering. Reindeer seem to know that people are their friends and protectors, Anna thought.

There was only one thing she could do. Gently she lifted the calf to her shoulders, his skinny new legs dangling down in front of her. He didn't struggle or protest but laid his soft chin on her head, ready for the ride.

This seems right, thought Anna. All her life, on the long trips to new grazing camps, reindeer had given rides to her and to her brothers and sisters when they were too tired to walk. Now Anna had a chance to give this little deer a ride to a new home.

The walk back to camp seemed long. As small as the little deer was, he was a heavy load on her shoulders. The eagle was nowhere in sight.

He must have decided that a deer and a girl were too much for even such a big bird to handle, Anna thought.

When Anna reached the camp, her two younger sisters ran to meet her. Inside their tent, she placed the calf gently on the dirt floor next to the glowing embers of the cookfire. The small girls cooed over the calf.

The calf looked very comfortable in his new home. He fell asleep beside the fire while the little girls stroked his back. At first only the soft, sleepy breathing of the calf and an occasional crackle from the fire broke the silence. Then in the stillness Anna heard a familiar whir and flap outside the tent. Quietly she went outside. A dark spread of wings was silhouetted against the sky.

"You may as well go hunting supper elsewhere, Old Man Eagle. Our calf has a home, and he's safe with his new family." Anna's voice floated on the still afternoon air. As if he had heard and understood, the eagle soared away over the hills.

Hot-Air Balloon Boy

By Denise Yannone

Chris's stomach rose into his throat as the hot-air balloon rose. "Dad, help!" he screamed.

Chris had climbed into the balloon's basket in preparation for the flight with his dad. But the air in the balloon was hotter than they realized. The balloon began to lift skyward before his father could jump into the basket.

"Pull the descent cord!" his father yelled.

Chris grabbed for the descent cord, but in his panic he accidentally pulled hard on the burner cord. The roar of the balloon's gas burner pounded in his ears. Flames shot out of the burner, which hung beneath the balloon's opening. Hot air filled the rainbow-striped balloon and pushed it up toward the clouds. A strong air current caught the balloon and propelled it even higher. There was no turning back.

Chris's knuckles turned white as he grabbed the rim of the basket. The familiar feel of the leather steadied him. Chris had flown dozens of times with his father, but he had never flown solo. And now he couldn't go back, and he couldn't land in the woodlands below. Chris had no choice. He must pilot all by himself to their regular landing spot, a large field due east of the launch site and south of the interstate highway.

Chris tried to remember to do the things his father had taught him. He checked the fuel gauge on the propane tank as he had seen his father do. The gauge read three-quarters full: enough fuel to carry him to the landing spot. The altimeter read 1,500 feet. Chris pulled on the burner cord again. The burner's roar shattered the quiet. Higher and higher he soared. I can do it, thought Chris. I can fly!

For the first time, Chris looked around. He could see green hills in the east outlined by the sunrise. A blaze of orange and yellow splashed across the blue sky. Even though air currents whipped around outside, from inside the basket everything felt calm.

Chris trained his binoculars on the ground. He saw fields polka-dotted with houses and barns. How far away I am, he thought. Everything looked like miniatures from a fairy tale. Chris felt as if he owned it all. It was a perfect flight.

Then a moving object below caught his eye. That must be Dad and Mike tracking me in the pickup truck, Chris decided. The red vehicle moved with him, zigzagging over the back roads and heading toward the open country.

His brother Mike was driving the truck. Mike was a permanent member of the ground crew. He would help fill the balloon with hot air and untether the ropes for takeoff. Then he would jump into the truck and trail the balloon to the landing spot. As it landed, Mike would secure the balloon. Then the balloon would be packed onto the truck, and Mike would drive home. "I like to keep my feet on the ground," Mike always said. Not me, thought Chris as he sailed across the sky.

Chris realized he wasn't alone anymore. A honking flock of wild geese flew beneath him.

The river below was a black licorice twist snaking its way across the Pennsylvania farmlands. The fields looked like patches from his mother's prize quilt.

Suddenly Chris lurched against the basket as the balloon arced sharply.

He pulled out the compass, and his eyes locked on the pointer. No longer did it find a home on top of the *E*. Instead, the pointer wiggled atop the *Northwest* heading. The wind had changed. Chris leaned over the edge of the basket. Like an invisible magnet, the wind pulled the balloon away from the regular landing spot and directly toward the interstate highway!

The fuel gauge measured less than a quarter tank. Chris knew he had to pull the descent cord or risk a crash landing. The lighter-than-air feeling left him, and a leaden weight tightened his muscles. I've been kidnapped by the wind, thought Chris. What if I can't overshoot the interstate?

Hoping to piggyback an air current that would carry him back to the landing spot, Chris tugged on the descent cord. The mouth of the balloon opened wide, spitting out hot air. The balloon fell smoothly, but the wind held its grip. Chris couldn't change direction.

The pickup truck had stayed with him, racing along the back roads. They're really moving, thought Chris as a trail of dust swirled out from behind the truck, but if they don't catch up with me, I won't be able to land. Someone has to grab the tether line, or the basket might bounce back into the air.

A bright red *E* glared out from the fuel gauge. "I'm out of fuel!" Chris gasped. He pulled harder on the descent cord. "I won't be able to fly over the highway." He stared down at the black ribbon of the interstate. Cars and trucks zoomed past.

The pickup truck finally reached the highway and tore out ahead of the balloon. Chris could see his father jump from the cab and race onto the roadway. He stopped traffic in one direction, while Mike jumped the median and brought the other lanes to a halt. They're clearing a landing pad for me, thought Chris.

"I'm out of fuel!" he yelled.

"Don't worry," his father called. "You can land here."

"Throw out the tether line!" shouted Mike. "We'll catch you." Chris jettisoned the heavy rope.

Mike lunged for the dragline and grabbed hold. He reeled in the rope as if it were a fishing line.

"Yank the descent cord all the way!" screamed his father. "Do it *now!*"

Chris tugged hard on the cord, and the top of the balloon yawned like a great whale. The basket thumped and bumped along the ground. Mike and Chris's dad anchored the basket, and the deflated balloon fell around them like a melted rainbow.

Horns honked, and drivers cheered and clapped. Chris had landed safely right in the middle of the busy interstate highway!

"Quite a big rainbow trout I caught," Mike said with a laugh.

Chris just grinned. "When's our next flight, Dad?" he asked.

"Just as soon as the wind is right, Chris," his dad promised. "And believe me, next time we'll fly together!"

Crow Know-How

By Eva Brown

"David! Where are you?" Debbie yelled. Her younger brother had been running downhill ahead of her. Now he was gone, with nothing in sight but manzanita bushes. She called again, "David, where are you?"

"Down here! I slid into a hole."

Debbie crossed a little ridge and braked to a stop just in time. There was David at the bottom of a deep hole. "Are you hurt?"

"Not too much. I sort of slid down the side."

"I'll go for help," Debbie told him.

"Won't you try to get me out first? You know how Ron is. He always treats me like a baby."

Debbie understood what David meant about their older brother. But how could she get David out alone? There was nothing here—no rope, not even a vine. "I'll have to go get a rope," she said.

"Wait. I have an idea," David said. "Tie our jackets and my belt into a rope." He tied his belt around his jacket and threw them up to Debbie.

As she tied jackets and belt together, Debbie thought about how this first visit to their grandparents' new home was turning out. Their family had come for Thanksgiving. Then she and her brothers had stayed for the weekend. "You think Gramps knows about this hole?" she asked.

"No, or he would never have let us come down here alone," David answered. Their "rope" ready, Debbie lay down and lowered it into the hole. "Oh, no," David wailed. "It's too short."

Debbie sensed his despair. He looked small down there, and helpless. Yet he was so brave— she had to try harder. An idea hit her, and she scrambled to her feet, pulling up the jackets. "Move to the far side, and watch out. I'm going to play crow."

"Play crow?" David jumped back as Debbie began dropping rocks, clods, and even chunks of wood into the hole.

"Remember the old fable?"

Her brother was too busy dodging to answer. As the rocks and clods began piling up, he caught on. "You're raising the bottom of the hole, aren't you?"

"Right. Now you pile it up to stand on."

When David was ready, Debbie lay down and lowered their homemade rope again. She braced herself. "Can you reach it?"

"Just barely. If you can get more stuff, it will work."

"If I can get more stuff . . . that's the problem," Debbie said as she pulled up the jackets. "I'll have to go farther out. I've gathered everything close."

"Don't get lost," David warned.

"I shouldn't. You can see the house through the bushes."

David laughed. "Maybe *you* can see the house. All I can see is sky."

Debbie walked and looked. Suddenly she spied a chunk of something black below her. It proved to be an old burned stump that had been grubbed out. She tried rolling it, but it got away and zigzagged downhill. She'd have to carry it. Now, which way was the hole?

"David, can you hear me?" she yelled. Surely she was not that far from him. Was something wrong? She tried to run. Unable to see over her load, she tripped and fell. This is no way to help David, she told herself as she got up. She looked up the hill. The house wasn't where it should have been. She moved to the left until the house lined up with the trees.

Again she called. This time she heard David's answer and hurried toward his voice.

"Where've you been? Did you get anything?"

"Yes. Get on top of the pile, and stand as close to the wall as you can."

Debbie put the stump down. Then she lay down and carefully lowered it over the edge.

"Wow! That should do it!" David yelled.

"Is it too heavy?"

"It's heavy, but I'll make it."

They tried their rope again. "It reaches!" David called. "Brace yourself. Here I come." Hand over hand, he climbed the jacket rope, digging his feet into the side of the hole.

With all her strength Debbie resisted being pulled into the hole. What a relief when David crawled over the edge. For a few minutes they rested. Then they jumped up and began beating the dirt off their clothes.

"Thanks for pulling me out, Deb."

"I didn't pull you out. You climbed out."

"But you helped me do that. Ron would have climbed down a rope and carried me out. I like your way."

They started toward the house, while Debbie untied their rope.

"What did you mean about playing crow?" David asked.

"Haven't you read the old fable? A thirsty crow found a pitcher with some water inside but couldn't reach the water. Then the crow had the idea of carrying pebbles and dropping them into the pitcher until the water came up high enough."

"So it was crow know-how that got me out," David said.

"Crow know-how plus teamwork," Debbie added.

THIS SIDE UP SHIP TO PHILADELPHIA

By Fran Pelham and Bernadette Balcer

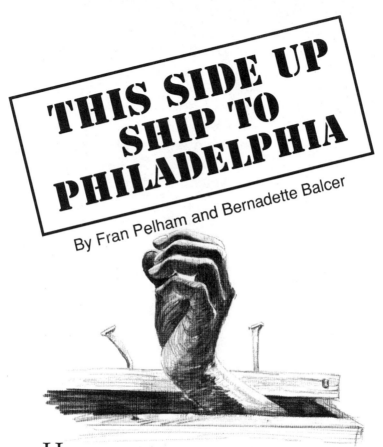

Henry Brown lay awake one night listening to the hum of the June bugs. Through the window of his wooden cabin, he saw tiny fireflies dancing in the blackness. Before he drifted into sleep, he heard one of the other slaves, Elijah, whispering: "I tell you, Mattie got *free*. He ran North. The dogs were yapping, but they never caught up." Henry fell asleep and dreamed of running away. He saw himself running free past the cotton fields.

When he woke up the next morning, Henry knew that running away was almost impossible. There were overseers with whips. There were sheriffs with bloodhounds and rifles. Runaway slaves got caught and beaten. No slave had ever escaped from the plantation where Henry lived in Richmond, Virginia.

But Henry didn't stop dreaming about running away.

One night a clever plan popped into his head. He needed a chance to make his plan work. On Saturday, Henry's overseer told him to take a horse to the town blacksmith. While the blacksmith was shoeing the horse, Henry visited a friend who lived not far from the blacksmith shop. The friend was Samuel Smith. Henry knew that Samuel was a "conductor" on a secret Underground Railroad that helped many slaves escape.

"Hello, Henry," called Samuel. "What can I do for you?"

"Samuel," said Henry, "can you build me a box? I need a box big enough for a person to fit into."

Samuel stroked his gray whiskers. "What do you have in mind, Henry?"

Henry replied, "I am going to get into the box

and you can ship me to Philadelphia. Then I will be free."

Samuel grinned. "It will have to be a small box, Henry. We don't want anyone to suspect there's a man inside."

Samuel and a few trusted friends built a strong wooden box, three feet long and two feet wide. They lined the box with straw.

The day finally came when Henry was to begin his adventure. That morning he ate cornmeal and a crust of bread for breakfast. He finished his chores in the stable, placing fresh hay, water, and oats in the stalls for the horses. Then, when no one was watching, he ran to the woods and headed toward Samuel Smith's house, about a mile away.

Samuel spotted Henry at the edge of the woods and waved him toward a red barn. "We must work quickly," Samuel said, leading Henry toward the crate. With one fast leap, Henry was inside the box. Samuel handed him a napkin filled with buttermilk biscuits. "My wife baked these for your journey," Samuel said. "Good luck," he added, then closed the lid.

Inside, Henry heard the pounding of the nails that sealed the crate. He felt the box shake as large straps were fastened around it.

Samuel's small daughter stenciled the words **THIS SIDE UP • SHIP TO PHILADELPHIA** in big block letters on the side of the box. On the top of the box, an address label read: "Mr. William H. Johnson, Philadelphia, Pennsylvania."

Samuel and two other men lifted the crate onto a cart and wheeled it to the railway office of Adams Express Line. "I'd like to ship this to Philadelphia," Henry heard Samuel say. Henry was careful not to cough or breathe too loud. In a short time, he felt himself roughly lifted and dropped onto a floor. He heard the hum of an engine. Soon a steady "toot-toot" assured him that he was on his way to Philadelphia.

Tiny holes had been bored into the side of the box so that air could circulate. The sweet scent of the fresh pinewood of the box filled Henry's nostrils. The *clackety-bang* of the train's wheels moving steadily over the tracks soon lulled Henry into a peaceful sleep.

Henry woke when the train screeched to a halt. He heard a conductor yell, "Fredericksburg!" A door to the baggage compartment slid open. Henry heard voices. Then, feeling two rough bumps against the side of the crate, Henry guessed more baggage was being loaded onto the train. Suddenly, Henry felt his box tip over. The blood rushed to his head. Henry began to feel the crushing weight of his body. He felt dizzy and sick. He couldn't moan.

In time, the train stopped again. More

baggage was flung against his crate. One large suitcase hit the edge of Henry's crate, knocking it upright. Henry said a silent prayer of thanks.

Twenty-six hours after he began his journey, Henry heard the happiest sound of his life: a conductor bellowing "PHILADELPHIA!"

Hours later, with Mr. Johnson's help, the crate reached the Anti-Slavery office. As Miller McKim, Lucretia Mott, and William Still unfastened the straps and nails on the box, they heard small groans. Lifting the lid, they saw a man, bent up like a pretzel, smiling at them.

Henry jumped up and said, "I sure am glad to be here." Soon after he became known as Henry "Box" Brown.

S O S

By Karla Anderson

Cheryl frantically adjusted the dials on the marine radio. She needed help quickly. Calm down now, she thought. I'm miles from shore and the only person who can get help for Dad.

She picked up the microphone. Her hands were damp, and it slipped from her grasp. Cheryl picked it up again. Dad had said that in case of an emergency on the ocean one should always call the Coast Guard.

She pushed the button on the microphone. "Calling San Diego Coast Guard," she said clearly. There was no response. She called again, then quickly took her finger off the call button.

"This is San Diego Coast Guard. Go ahead," came the answer.

Her father groaned from the bunk where he was lying. Cheryl pressed the button again. "I need help. My father and I are out on the ocean, and he's really sick. He keeps passing out."

"Stay calm," the voice said. "What is your name, and how old are you?"

"Cheryl Deering, and I'm ten." Her voice quivered. It was so good to know someone could hear her. All around the little boat the ocean was pitch black. No moon or stars shone. Cheryl was afraid.

The friendly radio voice came back on. "Cheryl, I need to know your boat's name, size, and color."

"It's the *Donnie Rae*. It is about thirty-two feet long. It's a white salmon-fishing boat with tall outriggers," she managed to blurt out in a trembling voice.

"Good. Don't break down now. We need your help. Where were you fishing?"

Cheryl took a deep breath. Think now. What

had Dad said? The something . . . Mile Bank. A number. The same number as Grandpa's age. "Dad said we were going to fish near the Sixty-Mile Bank," she replied.

"Great. That will put us somewhere in the general area. We may not be able to find you before daylight, but we will get there as fast as we can. Be sure you both have life jackets on. I'll call back soon."

Cheryl shone the flashlight on her father's face. He was so pale, and there were beads of dampness on his forehead. "Dad, can you hear me?" she called. No answer. She turned off the light and slumped on the floor with her head against the bunk and let the tears fall.

Sometime later she felt a hand touching her hair, and Cheryl jumped up. Her father was awake.

"Help is coming, Dad. Will you be okay?"

"I think it's appendicitis," her father whispered. "My right side hurts terribly, and I'm so hot."

"What can I do to help you, Dad?"

"A blue packet . . . in the emergency kit. Hit the packet hard against a flat surface, and it will get very cold. Place it against my right side to ease the pain." Cheryl did as she was told.

The radio called her. "How is your father doing now?" the man asked.

"He's awake but in a lot of pain. He thinks he has appendicitis."

"The patrol boat is on its way. There is a medical technician on board, and it should be in your area by the time the sun comes up. We have also dispatched a search plane. Do you have a bright light on board?"

"I have a big flashlight," Cheryl replied. "Also, the boat lights will run off the generator."

"Okay. Listen for the sound of a plane engine overhead. If you hear anything, signal."

"Yes, sir. You can count on me," Cheryl said proudly.

Her father was asleep now, and Cheryl felt very small and alone again. The little boat drifted as it tossed on the dark waves—up and down. She looked out the window. Nothing but salt water. To the east there was a slight touch of pink light. The sun was coming up. She was cold. She put the extra sleeping bag over her father, then wrapped herself in an old rain slicker and sat on a seat by the window to wait.

It seemed like a very long time until the radio called her again. Cheryl answered.

"Cheryl, the patrol boat and plane should be somewhere in your area now," the voice said. "Light up all of your lights, and listen and watch carefully. If you hear an engine, shine your flashlight toward the sound."

Another hour passed. Nothing. The sun came up. Suddenly in the early morning light Cheryl saw the search plane. She grabbed an old orange tarp and ran out on deck, waving it up and down. The plane passed over once, and Cheryl thought they had not seen her. Then it circled and returned.

"They're here, Dad. They're here," she yelled.

She ran to the radio and called her friend. "They've found us!"

"I know, Cheryl, they just radioed your position to me, and the Coast Guard patrol boat should be with you within a half hour. Meanwhile the plane will keep you in sight. You're a brave girl, and I'm going to be at the dock to shake your hand when you return to port."

Cheryl turned to see her father smiling weakly. "Everything is going to be all right now, honey, thanks to you. You can be my fishing partner anytime."

Breakup

By Marie Delilah Ward

Jake heard it first. Was it thunder? No, the sky was blue. Only one puffy white cloud hung above the thick ice on the Yukon River. The thunder came again. A big smile came to Jake's face.

"Jake, did you hear that?" Sam called. Sam was Jake's best friend. They had been friends all their lives and next year would be together in Fairbanks, the nearest city with a high school. Sam ran down the path from a row of houses.

"It's going to be a big one," Jake said. "Come on. Let's go up to the point."

The two boys climbed to the top of a hill, where they could see upriver. "Breakup! Breakup!" they called down to the village. This was what all the people were waiting for.

Cracks spread across the field of ice. Both boys jumped as the noise got louder and louder. The people on the bank were shouting, but the boys could barely hear them.

"Wowee!" shouted Jake as a slab of ice shot into the air and came crashing down. Other jagged pieces rose out of the white mass. They banged into each other like fighting monsters. The people standing close to the river began running back from the bank, but it was too late. A giant wall of ice pushed up the beach, and water shot into the air. It came down in a cold spray. The people were soaked. Everyone laughed, even those who had gotten wet.

Whole trees floated in the swift water. Chunks of earth rode on top of ice slabs.

Suddenly, Jake saw something else coming downriver on the ice. It wasn't a tree, but he couldn't be sure what it was. "Let's get a better look," he said to Sam, pointing upriver.

They ran along the trail to another high point. The dark spot came at them quickly, and soon they could see it clearly.

"It's a dog hitched to a sled," Sam yelled. But Jake was already running down to a sharp bend in the river. Sam followed.

On the floating chunk of ice, a beautiful white husky with a bushy tail howled sadly. It was strapped to a sled as the lead dog, but there was no sign of any other dogs. The trapper was gone, too. Maybe, Jake thought, the trapper had gotten all the dogs but one unhitched before the river split apart. The sled was loaded with furs.

Jake thought the ice chunk holding the dog might bump against the ice jam at the bend in the river. But even if it did, would the dog be too scared to jump onto the jam?

"Hi, big fella," Jake began to call. He and Sam had climbed far out on the risky ice jam. Jake hoped that talking to the dog would calm it.

"If it floats all the way down past the trading post, someone will shoot it for sure," Sam said. The boys had seen this happen before with a moose, caribou, or fox caught on the ice. An animal drifting on an ice slab with no food would suffer a slow death. It might be better to give it a quick end.

The ice slab caught in the rush of water heading for the jam, just the way Jake had hoped. He opened the blade on his pocketknife and shouted at the dog. "Come, boy. Hike! Hike!"

The dog forgot its fear when it heard the order. All its life it had obeyed orders at once. That was how it had become the lead dog. The strong husky leaped. It landed at Jake's feet, but the long straps that had held its team pulled it backward. It slid back. Its toenails would not hold on the icy wall.

Jake fell forward and got hold of a strap, but then he began to slip, too. Sam was able to get his hands around one of Jake's boots. Then he got the other foot in a good grip. He sank his own feet into the snow and ice.

By now the husky was halfway into the water. Working fast, Jake put the blade of his knife under one strap. It cut through. Pulling on the dog, he got the knife under the other strap. The ice slab with the sled broke away suddenly and went crashing downriver.

Without the pull of the sled, the husky's paws caught better on the ice. Its back feet found an ice step somewhere under the water. Jake held it by its long fur, and together they crawled onto flat ice.

Before the dog and Jake were all the way on their feet, the ice jam tipped. "It's giving way!" Sam shouted.

The boys leaped onto steady ice, then climbed

quickly to the safety of the bank. There was no time to think of the dog, but they didn't need to. Right at their heels was the beautiful snow-colored husky.

Jake gave the dog a big hug and got a lick on the cheek.

The dog barked happily.

"What will we call it?" Sam asked.

"It's a breakup dog," said Jake. "Let's call it Breakup."

"Come on, Breakup. Here, Breakup," the boys called. "Let's see if we can find your owner."

The husky wagged its tail and followed its new friends home.

You'll Never Make It!

By June Swanson

Jan Duncan's fingers trembled as she hurriedly wound the fishing line around the tops of two small willow trees. "There! That'll hold those two together. Now I'll bend that third one over and get it tied in."

She glanced nervously at her father's unconscious body. What a thing to happen! She was sorry she had ever suggested that they go fishing this afternoon. Anxiously Jan eyed the darkening sky. "I hope I can finish this shelter before it starts raining—have to keep Dad dry while I go for help."

Dad was always warning everybody about fishing from mossy rocks and logs, and now *he* had been the one to slip and fall! Jan hadn't actually seen the fall. She had heard Dad yell, but by the time she got there, Dad was lying on the bank, unconscious.

Jan's first thought had been to pull Dad up to the car, but she remembered something he had said once when they stopped at an accident on the highway. "Never move people who are hurt. They may have something broken, and you could make it worse. Just try to keep them comfortable until help arrives." It was then Jan remembered the gas station a mile or two back, where they had turned off the main road.

Now Jan finished tying the last of the willows together over Dad. Over the willow frame, she placed the poncho she had brought along. Grabbing her knife, she cut four short pieces of fishing line and tied the corners down. Even before she had finished tying the last knot, large drops of rain began to fall. At least it would be dry inside for Dad. Now she had to get to that gas station.

Pulling the collar of her windbreaker as far as it would reach over her head, Jan ran up the slippery path to the road. Rain stung her face. She could barely keep her eyes open, but she kept running. At last she could make out the shape of a building through the gray rain.

Shaking the water from her hair and clothes, Jan opened the door of the gas station. "Please, may I use your phone?" she asked breathlessly. "My dad's hurt."

A man behind the counter nodded toward the phone on the desk.

Jan grabbed the receiver, but there was no sound. She pushed the receiver button several times. Nothing happened. "I think something's wrong with the phone," she said.

The man took the receiver and listened. "You're right. It's dead. The storm must have knocked it out."

"Oh, no!" Jan cried. "My dad needs an ambulance." She began shaking, both from her wet clothes and from her feelings of fright and helplessness. "I'll just have to run to town."

"That's almost fifteen miles," the man said. "You'll never make it. Sit down a minute and tell me what happened."

The man listened intently as Jan explained about the accident. "Tell you what," he said when Jan had finished. "I probably won't have much business during this storm. I can drive you into town."

"Oh." Jan sighed. "That would be great! But, sir," she hesitated a second, "do—do you think maybe you could go and get the ambulance, and I could run back and take care of Dad?"

"Good idea," agreed the man. "Just tell me where your dad is and I'll get an ambulance there."

Quickly Jan gave him the directions. "Thanks

again," she called as she headed for the door. In a second, she was running back down the muddy road.

Her shelter was still dry inside, and Dad seemed the same. I better keep him warm, Jan thought. She cleared a place on the nearby bank, brushing away the wet leaves and pulling out weeds. There were waterproof matches in the tackle box. Dad had taught her how to build a fire in the rain. Jan tried to remember all the instructions. Finally a flame started, and she piled on the driest wood she could find.

As she watched the flames rise, the fear she had been holding back for the last hour rushed in on her. Had she really done the right thing? What if the man from the gas station had decided not to go to town? Was there something else she should be doing now? Jan strained her ears, hoping for a sound from the road.

The rain had stopped, and the woods were very still. The only sound came from the frogs croaking along the river. For the first time Dad moved and moaned. The movement sent shivers up Jan's back. What should she do now?

Just then she heard a far-off siren. Jan scrambled out of the shelter and up to the road. Now she could see the blinking lights of the ambulance. She waved her arms to get attention. As a woman and a man got out of the ambulance, Jan pointed and yelled. "My dad's down there!" They followed her down the hill and began to check Mr. Duncan.

After a few moments the woman said, "I can't find anything broken. It's probably a concussion." She glanced around. "Did you build this shelter? And the fire?"

Jan nodded.

"That's the best thing you could have done. You kept him warm and dry."

Jan sighed happily. She *had* done the right thing!

"It doesn't look like anything serious," said the man, "but we'll take him in to the hospital, anyway."

Jan was deep in thought as she gathered up the fishing poles and put out the fire. "What a strange day this has been. I never realized how much Dad has taught me—what to do in an accident, how to build a fire in the rain, and how to make a waterproof roof."

She smiled to herself.

The Unexpected Swimming Lesson

By Aure Sheldon

"Boy, we are early," said Craig sleepily. "There's not another person on the beach."

"Let's go out to that bar and look for sand dollars," Matt suggested.

At low tide the sandbar was easy to get to and seemed much closer than it really was. Craig followed his cousin as he threaded his way between the shallow tide pools on the exposed sand flats, stopping from time to time to examine strange forms of sea life stranded by the tide. There were sea urchins, jellyfish, and a dozen different kinds of sea snails.

As the dunes dropped farther behind them, Craig became more uncomfortable, yet he dared not admit it for fear that Matt would think him babyish. He was not at all sure of himself here. Although he had taken swimming lessons last winter, a swimming pool was one thing and the ocean was another. Secretly, he envied Matt, who was a strong swimmer and liked nothing better than to romp in the surf and ride the big waves into the beach. Craig began to wish that he had stayed in bed this morning instead of letting Matt coax him out to the water.

"Here's one . . . two . . . three!" shouted Matt. "Look, lots of them!"

The discovery of the sand dollars went far to dismiss Craig's fears. "Let's pretend they're real dollars and see who can find the most."

"I'll be a millionaire before breakfast time!" Matt laughed.

Absorbed by the race to "get rich quick," Craig followed Matt still farther out onto the sandbar. "Come and see this starfish," he called. "It has only three arms."

Matt stared at the wiggling starfish. "It's been

in a fight. Got a couple of them broken off."

"He can grow new ones though. That's some trick."

With so many fascinating things to see, time passed quickly. After a while, Matt dropped to his knees and said, "Let's count our dollars now and see who won."

"My shirt is almost full. I must have a million of them." Craig dumped out his sand dollars and began to count.

Another half hour or more passed as they counted their "money" and made rows of sand dollars in the wet sand.

Finally Matt sighed. "I'm hungry. Let's go back to the cottage and see if the others are up yet."

"It's getting hot anyway and . . ." Craig stopped abruptly. "Matt, look!" There was nothing but water between them and the shore.

"Sure, the tide's coming in," answered Matt matter-of-factly.

Craig wondered how Matt could be so casual. "What are we going to do?" he cried excitedly.

"Just get to shore before the water gets any deeper, that's all," Matt replied calmly. He gathered up his sand dollars and waded out from the sandbar toward shore.

"Wait! Wait a minute. I . . ."

Matt turned and said firmly, "No, don't wait. Come right now while you still can. I'll help you."

Craig was frozen to the spot. "I . . . I can't."

"Yes, you can," Matt reassured him. "Look, it isn't even knee-deep. But the longer you wait, the deeper it will be."

Try as he would, Craig couldn't bring himself to wade out into the water. "Matt, get my dad," he pleaded. "He can carry me across."

"What? By the time he gets here, that sandbar will be underwater too."

"Hurry, Matt!" Craig's voice cracked. "Please. I'm scared."

"All right, I'm going." Matt moved easily toward the shore, stopping only once to call back, "See? It's not even over my waist at the deepest part!"

Craig saw Matt reach the beach and set off on a dead run for the cottage, which nestled behind a low dune to the south. A flock of gulls flew low overhead, their hoarse cries sounding like mocking laughter.

He struggled for the courage to do as Matt had done. It had been so easy and so right. Yet he couldn't. If time seemed to stand still, the tide didn't. Anxiously Craig watched the sandbar grow narrower. He cupped his hands around his mouth and shouted desperately for help, but there was no one to hear him.

As he scanned the shore, a thin column of smoke above the cove to the north caught his eye. Rapidly, it thickened and grew dark.

"The boathouse is on fire!" he gasped. "Oh my gosh, there are gasoline storage tanks and lots of boats in there. I've got to get to a phone."

Without hesitating another moment, he waded off the sandbar and made straight for shore. At the deepest stretch, where the water came up to his chest, he kicked off strongly with his feet and swam. His father and Matt, running down the beach, saw him.

"You're swimming!" shouted Matt happily. "That's great. Keep it up!"

Craig came stumbling and sputtering out of the surf. "Call the fire department! The boathouse is on fire!"

One glance in that direction told them there was no time to lose. "Both of you run to the house and telephone for help," cried Craig's father. "I'll get over there and see what I can do."

The boys sped up the beach, Craig in the lead. He had always been a good runner, and he ran faster than ever now, for he knew he could do something else. He could swim. Anywhere.

Lost!

By Suzanne Rzeznikiewicz

It was a beautiful summer day. Nancy and her best friend, Carmen, decided to take a picnic lunch to Talcott Park.

"Be home before dark," said Nancy's dad, "and don't forget about using markings."

"What did your father mean by *markings?*" Carmen asked as they walked through the field and along the road that led to the park.

Nancy answered, "When we go on a hike, my dad marks the way we've gone by making a small pile of stones or bending a twig. He does this every hundred yards or so. Then if we lose our way coming back, we can look for the markings and follow them home."

They reached the entrance to the park and set off into the woods. The ground was damp from a rainstorm the day before. Here and there a flower poked its head up. When they stopped to watch a couple of squirrels chase each other around a tree, Nancy remembered to mark the spot with a pile of stones. They crossed a brook by hopping on rocks, and Carmen pushed a stick into the soft ground.

They saw a chipmunk run into a log and glimpsed a rabbit scamper through the trees. All along the way Carmen and Nancy left marks.

"Here's a good place for lunch," said Nancy.

They sat on a big rock. Nancy ate a turkey sandwich. Carmen had peanut butter and jelly. When they were finished, Carmen jumped up and tapped Nancy's shoulder. "You're it!" she called gleefully.

Carmen took off with Nancy chasing her. They giggled as they ran, turning this way and that way, between the trees. Suddenly Carmen slipped on some mud and sat down hard.

Nancy caught up with her. "Are you hurt?"

"Oh," groaned Carmen, "my ankle. I twisted it."

"See if you can stand," suggested Nancy. "I'll pull you up."

Nancy reached down and grabbed Carmen's hand. She braced herself and pulled as Carmen stood, leaning on her good foot.

Carmen said, "I can stand, I guess, but I'm not sure I can walk all the way home."

"Maybe I can find something for you to lean on," said Nancy.

She searched the ground around them and discovered a branch the right length to use as a cane.

"Nancy," said Carmen as she tried using the cane, "which way did we come? Everything looks the same around here."

"I don't remember either," Nancy said. "When we were running, I wasn't paying attention."

"I think we're lost," Carmen said with a worried expression.

"Wait," said Nancy. "Remember our markings? All we have to do is find them and follow them home."

The girls started walking slowly, Carmen using her cane and leaning on Nancy.

"I don't see any markings yet," said Nancy after they had gone a while.

"Me neither," Carmen replied. "Let's try a different way."

They changed direction and continued walking. A big dark cloud blocked out the sun. Nancy hoped it wouldn't start to rain.

"I think I see one," yelled Carmen. "Look, look. See the bent twig? I did that."

Nancy said, "Now at least we know we're going in the right direction. Let's keep looking for the next marking."

Farther on, Carmen and Nancy found another bent twig. Carmen was now able to put a little weight on her foot, and the girls picked up their pace.

"There's the brook." Nancy could see it between the trees.

"And there's the stick I used to mark where we crossed," Carmen said excitedly.

Nancy hopped across. Carmen followed, stepping gingerly on her bad foot.

"The next marking should be just a little farther," Nancy said with confidence.

They walked on until they saw the pile of rocks where they had watched the squirrels play.

"Now I know where we are!" Carmen exclaimed.

"Yes," replied Nancy. "My house is not far from here at all. I'm sure glad we used those markings. How does your ankle feel?"

"Not too bad," answered Carmen. "But all this

walking has made me hungry. We'll be home just in time for supper, and we'll have a good story to tell your dad."

Another Hunt

By Virginia Cowan

The slim, straight figure of a young Indian crossed in front of the fire and entered a skin tepee. Some moments later, a Sioux scout rode into the camp with news of having seen a herd of buffalo some miles to the south. There was much excitement in the camp, for it had been many suns since there had been a buffalo hunt.

The times now were few when great herds could be seen on the open plains. Without their sacred Tatanka to provide food and clothing, the people could not survive.

Inside the tepee, the young Indian, Little Wolf, settled himself on the soft skin rugs and watched his brother prepare for the morning's hunt. "It will be soon now, little brother," said Lone Eagle.

"Yes," replied Little Wolf, "it will be soon." He knew that the hunter must touch the buffalo before making the kill. This must be done with a coup stick made from wood and decorated with paint and feathers. Little Wolf had heard many stories in his father's lodge of the great herds and the counting of coup by the hunters.

Many winters before, when Little Wolf's father, Iron Hand, was a young man, he had touched the horn of the mighty Tatanka with his bare hand. This act of bravery had earned him the respect of his tribe. Tomorrow would be Little Wolf's first hunt, and his head was light with excitement. He hoped he, too, would bring honor to his father's lodge. Soon the young Sioux was asleep, dreaming of the hunt.

The sun had scarcely risen above the hills when Little Wolf arose. In his moccasined feet he walked silently about the tepee, gathering the things he would need for the hunt. He would take his best bow, sharp-tipped arrows, and his bone skinning knife. Some of the men would carry the white man's rifle, but Little Wolf was satisfied with his bow.

Soon all the camp was awake and stirring with the excitement of the hunt. Little Wolf was silent as he ate the pemmican his mother had prepared. He ate little, for he was too busy thinking of the hunt.

It seemed like forever to Little Wolf until the men finally mounted and gave the signal to leave. It was a good day for a hunt. The sun was hot, but there was a welcome breeze. The light wind felt good against Little Wolf's body as he rode.

They all rode bareback, and it wasn't long before they came upon the herd. The leader gave the signal to start the chase, and the men surrounded the buffalo. Little Wolf could feel the tension mounting, and for a moment he was afraid, but he overcame this feeling and galloped on with his heart pounding. He, Little Wolf, no longer a boy, rode with the men of the village on his first hunt. He was glad.

At first the buffalo were unaware of the approaching hunters; then the scent reached them and they broke into a run. Little Wolf's pony ran with the speed of an arrow, his feet scarcely touching the ground. Urging the horse closer and closer to the stampeding herd, Little Wolf could barely see through the cloud of dust. Suddenly there was a clearing, and as Little Wolf looked ahead his heart was gripped with fear. A lone rider lay on the ground only a few hundred yards from the stampeding buffalo.

There was only one thing to do, and Little Wolf kneed his pony, yelling "Hi-yi-yi!" The strong Indian pony obeyed the command instantly and within seconds was beside the fallen rider. With one quick motion, Little Wolf reached for the man's hand and pulled him to safety. He could see the gratitude in the man's eyes. He listened while the Indian told how his horse had stumbled in a hole and he had fallen to the ground, unable to move his injured leg.

Little Wolf also saw the pain in the injured man's face, and he recognized him now. He was called "The Wise One," for he had seen many seasons. The Wise One had once been the greatest of the buffalo hunters, and many came to hear his stories of the past. Little Wolf remembered how he, too, had come to hear these stories when he was younger. As Little Wolf looked at the man, he could tell how it pained him to move his leg, and he knew it would not be easy for him to ride. He knew that he should take the Indian back to his village and to his people.

All that could be seen of the herd was the cloud of dust left by the buffalo and the pursuing Indians. Little Wolf felt sick and sad. He had lost the chance of counting coup; he had lost the fun and adventure of the hunt; he had lost everything he had waited for so long.

The herd wasn't far off. It would be easy to catch up with the others. But it was Little Wolf's duty to take The Wise One back to the village, even if it meant giving up the hunt.

As the two rode on slowly, Little Wolf put the hunt from his mind. Then he turned the head of his pony to the north, and, as he did so, there was a feeling inside him that warmed his heart . . . there would be another hunt.

ROUNDUP

By Douglas Borton

Jill skimmed the reef at the edge of the fishery. The lights of the Ranch had nearly faded from view. She knew she wasn't supposed to be out this far alone, but Jill liked the feel of the minisub under her control. She saw her reflection in the window, lit from below by the instrument panel. Ahead she could see the thousands of whitefish that were this year's crop.

A good crop, her mom had said. The whitefish, along with the plankton and seaweed, might allow the Ranch to turn a profit for the first year ever. Just last winter her mom and Uncle Jorgens had been talking about selling and moving topside if things didn't work out.

Jill hadn't liked that. She was twelve years old, and she'd never been topside except for day trips when they took the crop to market or when her mom took her shopping for clothes. It was okay, she guessed, for some people—but the sea was her home. She'd been born and raised here, at the undersea colony everyone called the Ranch, and she didn't want to leave.

You couldn't see anything like *this* topside, she told herself proudly. The glittering schools of fish were spread out over the reef like a living carpet. They were called whitefish, but they weren't really white. They were yellow-brown on top and whitish below, with blue stripes edging their fins. Each was two or three feet long, twenty or thirty pounds—and delicious. Her mom liked to broil them and serve them on a plate of fresh-picked seaweed.

They were bred in the fishery, just as cows were bred in topside ranches. The fish were allowed to swim freely inside a giant plastic bubble a half mile wide.

Jill knew that in the old days people had gone

out in boats to catch fish. Sometimes they still did, but mainly for fun. It made a lot more sense to grow your food than to have to hunt for it. It was easier, and once you got the hang of it, it was cheaper, too.

She looked at the clock on the instrument panel. 6:15. Time to head back, she decided, before her mom started worrying about her. She pressed the joystick to the left, and the sub nosed around.

The rumbling caught her by surprise. At first she thought it was engine trouble. Then she saw silt rising off the sea floor and small rocks tumbling down in slow motion. An earthquake from the rift, she realized.

The Ranch was connected by seven miles of cable stretched across the ocean floor to a power generator. The generator used heat from a volcanic rift, converted it to electric current, and sent it through the cables to the colony. Uncle Jorgens and her mom had known it was risky to build so near the rift, but they needed power. Solar energy wouldn't work a hundred feet down, nuclear energy was too expensive, and batteries like the ones in the sub couldn't power a whole colony. So they had taken the chance.

The rumbling continued, low and ominous. Jill tapped into the sub's computer for information.

The quake measured 4.4 on the Richter scale. That didn't seem strong enough to do really serious damage. But—

As she watched, a long jagged fissure appeared in the plastic bubble that enclosed the fishery, then another, and another. Part of the bubble splintered into a crystal spider web as the reef below it trembled and shifted.

Panicked by the vibrations, whitefish streamed out through the cracks and scattered in a thousand directions.

Jill saw her future under the sea scattering with them. "Oh, no, you don't," she said. She rammed the joystick forward, and the minisub sped in pursuit.

The sub was used for hauling fish to stock the fishery. She had often sat right here, next to her uncle, as the sub dragged its nets along the ocean bottom. Scanning the controls, she found the button that released the first net.

The net ballooned out from the rear of the sub and expanded with the rush of water. Hundreds of whitefish were caught in its folds, like plankton scooped up in the mouth of a whale.

Jill guided the sub to the right. The sub's searchlight picked out more of the fleeing whitefish in the murky water, like yellow-white snowflakes against a night sky. She glided forward, closing in on them, and released the second net. She passed directly over the fish. The sub slowed down a little with the drag of the added weight in the net. She shifted to full power and felt the sub surge forward.

She turned and swept her searchlight over the bubble. It was nearly empty. She sped over the reef, skirting the bubble, as multicolored rocks and twisting strands of seaweed rushed past her. Then clouds of silt disturbed by the earthquake swirled up around her, cutting off her view. She pressed a button, and the computer showed a radar image of everything passing by. She used the computer image to guide her through the silt.

Past the reef the water was clearer. More whitefish were visible ahead. She released the third and fourth nets and guided the sub in wide circles, gathering up as many of the fish as she could find.

By the time she was done, the clock read 6:45, and the last low rumbles had ceased.

The nets were full. She had saved at least three-fourths of the crop. The Ranch could still make a profit. They wouldn't have to sell and move topside. Not this year, anyway. Not ever, if Jill had anything to say about it.

She pointed the sub toward the Ranch. Its lights glowed faintly in the distance. About halfway home she saw a brighter light approaching out of the murk. Another minisub. She made radio contact.

"Jill!" There was anger and relief in her mom's voice. "Are you all right? We've been looking everywhere! What are you doing out this far?"

"Just fishing," said Jill. She smiled and told her mom and uncle about the crop that almost got away.

The Dive

By Ellen Lewis

Yousuf waited for the pain. He knew it would come.

"Ouch!" he cried.

"Stop the whimpering, boy," the wrinkled old man said sharply. "You will get used to it in time."

Then he held Yousuf's head in his strong, dark arms and pushed the *fitam* tortoise-shell noseclip onto Yousuf's nose.

The old wooden boat rocked gently in the sparkling waters of the Gulf. Yousuf breathed slowly through his mouth as the old man gave him the choice.

"Look here. Which will it be, boy?" the old man said. "The tar or the cloth?"

Yousuf looked down at the deck. His eyes looked from the can of sticky tar to the piles of white cotton cloths.

"Either one will help keep the sharks and stingers away, boy," the old man said. "They don't much like the taste of either." He chuckled.

Yousuf looked around quickly at the experienced divers. Some wore the lightweight cotton trousers and hooded top, while others preferred the tar. He made his choice.

The old man scooped a handful of greasy tar from the tin and began to spread it on Yousuf's arms and legs. His skin tingled for a few minutes as he stood and watched the others.

The older divers on the pearling boat knew what to do, and Yousuf felt envious. They tied their loincloths around their waists and legs. Then they looped a rope with a heavy stone attached to it around one ankle. The stone would help them sink rapidly to the seabed. An oyster basket, attached to the lifeline rope, hung from the other ankle. The dagger, used to cut through soft coral, was held between their taut bodies and the loincloth. Those who used the tar stained their skin every day, applying the grease without thinking. Those in cotton dressed quickly and tied their hoods.

Suddenly the song leader, Nahham, beat the drum. His strong, clear voice cried, "Oh, Allah . . . may we be fortunate today."

The songs of the pearldivers began. Yousuf listened to the haunting pleas, and he knew that someday he would know all the songs. He would know the *Nehma* as well as all the other divers, who sang the words as they carried out their tasks.

The first divers leaped off the side of the boat, splashing into the water with such grace that the surface was hardly disturbed.

Yousuf watched as the brown figures slipped beneath the sea. He stared at their only trace— the wriggling ropes tied to the boat.

It seemed to Yousuf that an hour passed as he waited for the men to return from the deep.

How strange, he thought. Down there, wedged among the rocks and stones, is my family's food . . . clothing . . . the camel . . . the medicine. And all from one tiny speck of nature, one raindrop swallowed by the oyster. The pearl. Somewhere in the West men pay great sums for the pearls of the Gulf. He smiled. The pearl is my gold.

"Yousuf!" cried the old man. "Stop the daydreaming. You're next."

"Sorry. Sorry," he muttered. He moved near the edge of the boat. The first divers emerged from the deep, red-faced and with baskets full of the precious oysters.

The sun was burning them all, but Yousuf felt cold. He was afraid.

"Come! Come!" cried the old man. He sounded impatient.

The others were crouched on the narrow deck, tearing open the oysters in search of their bounty. No one noticed Yousuf.

He tightened his ropes and breathed deeply a few times. He stood with his fellow divers, toes curled on the edge of the old boat.

"Ready?" shouted the old man.

He pushed the oiled cotton into his ears. The singing seemed far away now. He filled his lungs as deeply as he could.

Not too deeply, he thought.

Don't breathe too deeply or you'll faint. He touched his dagger. It was secure. He checked his basket. His heart pounded.

He glanced down at the water, so clear, so harmless, so inviting.

"Now!" cried the old man, as he had done for almost a lifetime.

Feet first, Yousuf slipped through the cool water. Down, down to the reef, a mere breath away from his fortune.

A Cry for Help!

By Mary Jane Biskupic

Kathy's dad had been transferred again. Kathy would have to change schools and leave the friends she had made. But this time the transfer was different. The family would be going to Germany.

Mother decided the family should learn to speak as much German as possible in the time before their move. She made up a game. The kitchen would be Germany, and only German would be spoken there. The family could speak whichever language they wished in the other rooms of the apartment. What started out as fun soon became a problem for Kathy.

"*Guten Morgen!*" Kathy's mother said, bidding her good morning.

"*Guten Morgen,* Mother."

"*Mutter,*" she corrected her.

She was "Mother" in the rest of the house, but in the kitchen she was *Mutter.*

Kathy drank her orange juice and ate her pancakes. She wanted more but didn't know how to ask in German. Mother wouldn't help. She pretended she didn't understand her English and kept saying "*Ich verstehe nicht.*" ("I don't understand.")

Kathy went to school without having any more pancakes. She decided that she ought to learn a few more German words before supper—especially words for dessert.

Her friends at school listened to Kathy tell about the plane her family would take to Germany. She tried to sound more excited than she felt because she didn't really want to leave Maplebrook School.

After school the librarian found a book that would help Kathy learn German. *Kuchen* was the word for "cake." She knew she'd better say *bitte*, too, because her mother insisted that she say "please" no matter what language she spoke. If she didn't eat anything but cake for supper, Kathy would be happy. And now she had a book to look up the right German word for whatever she wanted to say.

Uh oh! thought Kathy as she came in the front door. Mom's in the kitchen.

She greeted her with a flow of German that Kathy didn't understand. Mom always asked her how things went in school, so Kathy hoped that was what she had just said and replied, "*Gut*."

During the next several weeks Kathy learned fast. Sometimes she spoke German when she wasn't in the kitchen. Once she said *Fahrrad* instead of "bike" when she was playing with her friend Tony.

One day she rode her *Fahrrad* to Tony's house to see if Tony was through delivering his newspapers and could play. As she passed the big apartment building on the corner, Kathy heard her name and saw Tony waving from the doorway.

"Hey, Kathy, come here quick! I think someone's hurt."

Kathy dropped her bike by the bushes and ran inside with Tony.

"I was walking past this door, and I heard

someone moaning. I called to him, but I can't make out what he's saying, and the door's locked," Tony gasped as they stopped in front of one of the apartment doors. "Listen–maybe you can understand him."

With her ear to the door, Kathy heard, "*Bitte . . . Ich kann mir nicht helfen . . . Beinbruch.*"

"I think he's got a broken leg," Kathy said. She thought for a moment and then shouted, "*Wir bringen Hilfe.*"

"What did you say?" asked Tony.

"I told him we would get help," Kathy explained. "Try those apartments down the hall. As soon as we find someone home, we can call the rescue squad."

After trying three apartments, Tony finally got someone to answer the door and let him use the phone. He dialed the emergency number, told the operator what was wrong, and gave him the address of the building.

The ambulance got there in about ten minutes, but they seemed like the longest ten minutes ever. Kathy had tried to say that help was on its way, but she couldn't get the man inside to understand.

The paramedics broke open the door and began asking the man questions as they examined him.

"*Ich verstehe nicht*" was all the man said.

"Maybe I can help. I speak a little German," Kathy said.

"Good. You two come along with us. Looks like this fellow took a nasty fall. He may have a concussion and some broken bones," one of the medics said.

Later, when their patient was being treated in the emergency room, one of the paramedics thanked Kathy and Tony for their help. "Tony, you could have just walked away and not done anything. It took courage to help Mr. Schmidt. And, Kathy, you sure helped out by knowing German. What was it you told him?"

"My mother made sure we learned the word for 'doctor' in case we ever needed one," Kathy replied. "I just told him *Er ist Arzt* . . . that you were a doctor."

It was only a few days later that Kathy's dad came home and said he had some bad news.

"My orders have been changed. We aren't going to Germany."

"Great!" cried Kathy.

"Kathy, I thought you'd be disappointed after having learned to speak German."

"No, Dad! I don't want to leave my friends. But Mom's idea about learning to speak German was good. Let's pretend you're transferred to France, Dad. I'd like to learn some French."

How to pronounce the German words
in this story:

good morning—Guten Morgen
(GOO-tn MOR-gn)

mother—Mutter (MOO-tr)

I don't understand.—Ich verstehe nicht.
(ikh fer-SHTAY-eh nikht)

cake—Kuchen (KOO-kn)

please—Bitte (BIT-eh)

good—Gut (goot)

bicycle—Fahrrad (FAR-rahd)

I can't help myself.—
Ich kann mir nicht helfen.
(ikh kahn meer nikht HEL-fen)

broken leg—Beinbruch (BINE-brookh)

We are bringing help.—Wir bringen Hilfe.
(veer BRING-n HIL-fe)

He is a doctor.—Er ist Arzt. (air ist artzt)

Overboard!

By Arthur M. Winer

"Look out, Dad!" I screamed. The wind tore my words away as I clung to the wheel of our 32-foot sailboat. An enormous wave was sliding under the boat just as Dad was letting go of the handrail.

My terrified warning came too late. *Windsong* rolled to starboard, and Dad lost his footing on the wet foredeck. He fell over the lifelines and into the sea!

As he disappeared under the water, I froze with fear until he burst to the surface in *Windsong*'s wake. All the things Dad had taught me to do if someone went overboard spun through my mind. But I couldn't remember what I was supposed to do first. Meanwhile *Windsong* charged ahead, leaving my dad farther behind.

Tears stung my eyes, and I felt seasick, but some instinct made me turn the wheel, bringing the boat's nose into the wind. The sails began cracking like giant whips, but gradually *Windsong* lost way and stopped.

I left the wheel and pulled the horseshoe buoy out of its rack. I threw it as hard as I could in my dad's direction, but it fell far short. When I tried to lift the man-overboard pole out of its tube, I found it was jammed. I was still struggling with the pole, crying with frustration, when to my horror *Windsong* started to sail again. I jerked the wheel over and released the lines to both sails. Now, no matter which way the boat turned, the sails would not fill.

Swimming against towering waves, Dad had managed to reach the horseshoe buoy. Using it as a float, he began kicking toward the boat. He was tiring quickly, but I shouted at him to keep swimming. Finally he was alongside, exhausted and shivering.

I reached down and tried to help lift him over

the railing but almost went over myself. His clothes, soaked with water, must have added another fifty pounds to his weight.

"It's no use, Lee. I can't get into the boat."

"Hang on, Dad. Please!" I begged.

Suddenly, I noticed that the line to the forward sail was trailing in the water.

"Dad, grab the jib sheet, and tie it around yourself." He recognized immediately that I had found a way to bring him aboard. While he struggled to tie the line around his body, I wrapped the other end around the winch. Then I grabbed the winch handle and locked it in place.

I could crank in only a few inches of line at a time, but slowly I lifted my father up the side of the boat. Now he was able to reach up and grip the cockpit railing. As the boat dipped to the next wave, he rolled under the lifeline and fell into the cockpit.

For a long time we just held each other. When Dad finally stumbled below to change into dry clothes, I managed to start the engine. We just let the sails flog all the way back to the harbor entrance.

As we motored up the last channel, Dad put his arm around my shoulder. I felt a special unspoken bond between us—something more than the love that had always been there. The sea had tried to take Dad, but I had fought back. I knew the next time I went out on the ocean I would look at it differently, with more respect but also with new confidence.

Maybe that's why, as we stood side by side in the cockpit, I turned to Dad and asked, "Can we go sailing tomorrow?"

There was a long silence. Then he grabbed me in a bear hug and in a quiet voice said, "Of course we can."